Hats

written by
Deborah Williams

illustrated by
Dennis Graves

KAEDEN ❤ BOOKS™

Title: Hats
Copyright © 2017 Kaeden Corporation
Author: Deborah Williams
Designer: Laura McAlpin
Illustrator: Dennis Graves

ISBN: 978-1-879835-93-1 (paperback)
ISBN: 978-1-61181-667-9 (eBook)

Published by:
    Kaeden Publishing
    P. O. Box 16190
    Rocky River, Ohio 44116
    1-(800)-890-READ(7323)
    www.kaeden.com

Printed in the United States
W-7/2017

First edition 1997
Second edition 2001
Third edition 2013
Fourth edition 2014
Fifth edition 2017

Table of Contents

His **hat** is red.

Her hat is blue.

Yellow

Her hat is yellow.

His hat is white.

Her hat is black.

His hat is orange.

His hat is gray.

Her hat is green.

His hat is purple.

Who wears a hat that is red, yellow, blue, green, orange, and purple?

A **clown!**

Glossary

clown – someone who wears funny clothes and funny hats and tries to make people laugh

hat – a cover worn on your head

Index